Leopard Poachers

Written by Kathy Hoopmann
Illustrated by Donna Acheson-Juillet

Collins

D1458151

Chapter 1

"Ali, stop!" Sameer hissed. "Get down!"

The urgency in Sameer's voice made Ali obey instantly. He dropped to the rocky ground and peered around nervously.

"What?" he whispered to his brother.

"Leopard!" Sameer said quietly. He pointed over the next ridge.

Ali's eyes grew wide with wonder and fear. An Arabian leopard? They were almost extinct in this region. Their parents would never have let them climb the mountain alone if they'd known one was here.

"I want to see," Ali said, but Sameer shook his head.

"Too dangerous."

"Please. I'll never get another chance," Ali begged.

Sameer was torn. It was his job to watch out for his brother, but to see a leopard in the wild was so rare.

"OK," he relented. "Just a quick peek."

The two boys crept up to the ridge and peered over. The leopard stood on the edge of a cliff so close they could see it clearly. It was magnificent with greyish white fur with a deep golden yellow on its back, and the whole body blotched with black. Luckily the wind was blowing towards the boys, or the leopard would smell them for sure.

"It's hurt," Sameer whispered in Ali's ear and
pointed to the wound on its leg, which was raw
and festering. "Poor thing."

Suddenly, there was a *thoop* sound and the leopard
gave a roar of pain and stumbled before falling
to the ground.

Ali and Sameer stared at each other in shock.
Before they could move, two men came from behind
a huge boulder with guns under their arms. One man
was bald. The other wore a brimmed hat and had
a black beard. Sameer pulled Ali out of sight, but not
before he heard one man shout at them, "Hey you!"

"Run!" Sameer cried, and Ali didn't need to be told twice. He took off along the rugged top of the mountain. Sameer pounded behind him, panting with fear. Too fast! Ali's foot wedged in a crack. Falling heavily, he grunted in pain as his ankle twisted and his shins ripped against a rock, shredding skin.

A voice behind them yelled, "Wait!"

"Don't stop!" Sameer cried, as he scrambled past Ali,
dodging behind cragged outcrops, keeping out of sight
of the men. "They saw us!"

Ignoring the blood oozing from his cuts, Ali
struggled to his feet and followed his brother in his
mad dash down the mountain. Ali dislodged a rock
that catapulted down a cliff face. They would be heard
for sure. All the more reason to get away. Fast!

Then Sameer saw a hiding place. Two massive
boulders had tumbled together long ago to form
a small cave.

"Here!" Sameer wheezed. "We can rest a minute. Catch our breath."

Ali dived in and sprawled on the rocky floor, puffing like a camel after a race.

"We've got to stay out of sight," Sameer managed to say after a few minutes, as he took a sip from his water bottle, then handed it to Ali.

Ali took a sip and handed back the bottle. The boys lay on their tummies keeping as low as they could, straining to hear any noise that told them they were being followed.

Finally Sameer whispered, "They must be poachers. We've got to tell Mum and Dad."

"How could they shoot it?" Ali whimpered. "It was so beautiful."

"Leopard skins are worth a lot on the black market," Sameer replied.

Ali started to shake. And he wasn't cold. Midday in the desert was hot, even in winter, like it was now. "They must be crazy. Do you think they'll try to follow us?"

"If two kids saw you kill an endangered animal, would you follow them?" Sameer replied.

Ali's silence said everything. What were they going to do? Their camp was a two-hour walk away.

"We have to go down. Just as well we came up the mountain this side," Sameer said. "I bet they think it's too steep for us. They'll expect us to go down the track, for sure."

He peered out of the cave, ears straining for sounds of danger. Everything seemed peaceful. Even a bird squawked overhead.

Suddenly, way too close, they heard a voice shout.

Ali stared, wide-eyed. "They're coming! What do we do?"

Sameer didn't know. But he couldn't tell Ali that. The oldest should always know what to do.

"Get as far back in the cave as you can," he said finally and they shuffled backwards. "They may go straight past us."

"And if they don't?"

"They will," Sameer said. They have to, he added to himself. The boys crouched still, scarcely breathing. Listening for the sound of their pursuers.

Suddenly Ali stiffened. "Did you touch me?" he whispered.

"No. What's the matter?"

Ali glanced behind them. An orange-brown snake slithered across the floor of the overhang, using Ali's foot as a speed bump.

"Don't move!" Sameer whispered. "It's a sand boa. It won't hurt you if you don't do anything to scare it."

"But it's scaring me!"

"Stop shaking!"

"I can't help it," Ali whimpered. He shook violently and the snake stopped. It turned lidless eyes on the boys. Ali couldn't take it any more. He bolted out of the cave, whacking his head on the rock as he went.

"Ali!" Sameer yelled.

Another second and both boys were gone.

Chapter 2

Sameer and Ali clambered down the mountain.

"Can you see them?" Ali called over his shoulder.

Sameer risked a backwards glance. There! High above them. A hat. But it was behind a rock. The man wasn't looking their way.

"Yes!" Sameer hissed. "Keep going. Quickly!"

They struggled on and on, down and down.

The spiny desert shrubs that grew out of nooks and crannies scratched at their faces and arms and legs. They slid and slipped and scrambled until the steep cliff face levelled to become a wadi; a waterless river bed. Stunted grasses and bushes grew along the edge where they would get water during the rare floods. The sun shone relentlessly overhead in a sky so hazy it was a yellow brown, rather than blue.

It was all too much for Sameer. His legs ached. He needed to stop and rest for a moment. He saw a tree growing in what seemed to be bare rock, and he collapsed to the ground aching for air. His ribs heaved but still he scanned the cliff for any sign of their pursuers. All was clear. Ali fell down beside him. A brisk breeze whisked the sand into little swirls and stung their faces, but the umbrella-like tree shade was a huge relief.

After a few moments, Sameer's heartbeat slowed enough for him to get some words out. "I thought ... you might ... need a rest," he panted.

"Yeah ... thanks," Ali puffed. "Have we lost them?"

"Dunno. We made a lot of noise. Listen."

They froze, willing their hearts to beat more quietly.

What was that? A clatter of rocks nearby made them stop breathing. Someone was close! Too close. There was nowhere to run. The noise came again from behind a clump of trees. Sameer pushed Ali behind him and tried to stand brave. Then he heard a bleat, and he and Ali grinned in relief. A wild goat emerged and stared at them curiously. Sameer shooed it, and it trotted away.

"Maybe the men will hear it and think it's us and chase it instead," Sameer said in hope.

Suddenly they heard another distant cry.

"Too late!" Ali hissed, his voice hoarse with fear. "They've found us!"

Sameer dragged Ali behind a bush with spiky branches and forced him down. But there were no cries from anyone chasing them. No thudding footsteps pounding closer.

"That cry could have been a long way away. Sound travels out here," Sameer whispered at last.

"You think?" Ali gulped.

They were silent for five long minutes, breathing in each other's dread. Perhaps they heard far-off shouts or maybe they heard the cry of a falcon, or the grumble of a camel.

Every sound was a threat. Each rustle hid a menace. The tension grew until Sameer thought he would scream.

"I guess we lost them," he said at last, willing it to be true.

Ali looked around at the unfamiliar area. "I think we've lost ourselves as well," he said, his voice small.

"It's OK," Sameer reassured him. "I've got my compass." He took it from his pocket. "That's north," he said, pointing across the wadi. "And that's south," he added after a long pause, pointing back up the mountain.

Ali nodded. "So which way is our camp? We've got to find Mum and Dad. We must tell the police what we saw."

Sameer frowned, staring hard at the compass. "Um, we have to go that way," he said, pointing to his right. "No, wait. That way." He pointed in the opposite direction.

"We're lost!" Ali groaned. "You don't have a clue where we are, do you?"

Sameer didn't know, but he just couldn't let his little brother down. He had to find a way to safety. "Come on," he said, getting to his feet. "Let's start walking. We'll be fine. Don't worry."

Ali got up too, and then saw something move on his brother's back.

"Sameer," he hissed, in a voice full of dread. "Don't move."

Sameer froze, hearing the fear in his brother's voice. "What is it?" he whispered back. He looked up the mountain thinking he would see a man with a gun coming towards them, but there was nothing.

"There's a massive, gigantic 'thing' on your back!"

"Ahhh!" Sameer whimpered in terror, standing statue still. "What is it?"

"It's pale and weird and has ten legs and it's bigger than my hand!" Ali said, staring at it in horrible fascination.

"A camel spider!"
Sameer shrieked.
"Get it off me!"
Ali grabbed
a stick from the
ground and was
about to whack
the spider as hard
as he could when
he realised Sameer
mightn't like that too
much. Instead, he angled
the stick under the spider and
then, with all his might, he flicked it away. The spider
flew into the air like a mutant
ten-legged bird. It thudded
against a rock ledge and
hit the ground with
a splat. Sameer turned
in time to see it
wobble a bit, then
scamper away behind
some boulders.

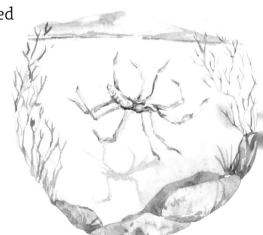

That animal was gigantic! And it had been heading for his neck! Sameer felt faint but didn't want to sit down in case its friend was lurking nearby.

"How can a spider have ten legs?" Ali asked, ready to run if the thing poked its head out again.

"It's not really a spider, but it's part of the spider-scorpion family. And it's not poisonous, but it can still bite," Sameer said. "Thanks for getting it off me, Ali. You did well."

Ali tried to smile at the praise and hide the tears in his eyes at the same time. His shins throbbed and he could feel the bruise on his head from bumping the overhang in the cave. He'd shared a cave with a snake, a monster spider-thing had hitched a ride on his brother's back, they were lost and they were being hunted by poachers. It really wasn't a good day. He sagged his shoulders and looked up at Sameer. "I wanna go home," he sniffed, wiping his nose on his shirtsleeve.

Chapter 3

Sameer stared at his brother. Ali looked dreadful and Sameer knew he was just as bad. "Come on," he said, "we've got to keep going. We'll come across something we recognise soon and find the camp."

"But what about the poachers? We can't let them see us!"

"We're way ahead of them by now." Sameer tried to sound confident. "And we can run faster than them if they do see us." He wondered if that was really true.

"I can't," Ali moaned.
"I'm beat."

Sameer felt terrible.
Everything he did, Ali
always wanted to try too.
It was annoying at times.
Today, when Ali had
insisted on climbing
the mountain with his big
brother, Sameer chose
the hardest path, the steep
track that he'd climbed
once before with his dad.
He knew the way, but he
also knew it would be hard
for Ali to keep up.
Big brothers rule, OK!

But now the rules had changed. They were lost.
They were in danger. And it was his fault. If they'd
stayed on the main track, they wouldn't have seen
the poachers. With a cringe of guilt, Sameer remembered
his mum's gentle smile as they left camp. "Watch Ali
for me," she'd said. He had to get Ali to safety.

"Listen," Sameer said finally. "I'll climb a ridge and see if I can spot the campsite. You stay here and rest." Ali nodded, but moved well away from where the camel spider had run.

Sameer scanned the area. They'd wandered into a deep valley. Steep cliffs were either side of them. There was no way he could climb up here. He was about to suggest they keep walking when he noticed that an old palm tree had blown over years ago, and its trunk made a bridge to a rock shelf. From there, he would be able to see out across to the sand dunes, and hopefully spot his camp. He jumped onto a boulder then leapt up onto the sideways tree, running along the trunk, higher and higher into the air. The gusty wind threatened to unbalance him.

Ali watched. Alone and vulnerable. "Wait!" he called. "I'm coming too!" He clambered over the boulder and crawled onto the trunk.

"Careful, Ali!" Sameer cried. "The tree's rotting in places." And just then, to prove what he said was true, Sameer's foot crunched through the bark and he had to grab the prickly trunk to keep from falling. He knocked his head on the rocks beside the tree and blood oozed out.

Then suddenly he gave an enormous yelp. "Yeeeeouch! Bees! I've just squashed their hive!"

Sameer wrenched his foot from the hole and wriggled back down the trunk, slapping his arms and face as he went.

Ali's heart raced. He stood numb with terror, watching the swarm around Sameer. Ali was allergic to bees. He always carried special tablets in case he was stung, but Mum kept them in her bag, and neither Mum nor her bag were here now. Too many stings and he'd be dead in minutes.

Sameer knew his brother was in danger. "Run!" he cried.

With a howl of fear, Ali jumped off the tree, scrambling down the boulder, and began to sprint as soon as his feet hit the ground. Sameer was close behind him.

They ran until the angry buzz was left well behind. They ran until they could run no more.

When they stopped, both boys were sobbing in pain. Sameer was covered in red lumps, and blood trickled down his face. Then he looked at his brother. Ali's right eye had already started to puff up.

"How many times were you stung?" Sameer asked.

"Only once," Ali blubbered. "If I'd been where you were ..." His voice trailed away as he looked at the bites all over his brother.

"We've got to get out of here," Sameer said in a tight voice. He looked around in desperation. The cliffs surrounded them, unhelpful and uncaring.

"Listen!" Ali said suddenly.
The chopping roar of a helicopter
thudded overhead.

Sameer frowned. "What's a helicopter
doing all the way out here?"

"Perhaps it's a search 'copter looking
for us!"

"No way," Sameer replied. "No one
knows we're lost, and Mum and Dad
aren't expecting us back for ages yet.
It must belong to the poachers."

They both looked up and saw
the helicopter disappearing in
the distance.

"It's really low," Sameer said.
"It must be going to land near here.
Let's follow it, but be careful. We don't
want to get caught."

With the last of their strength,
the boys broke into a slow jog and
followed the chopper's receding
clacking sound.

"Hey! There's a clearing!" Sameer said as the wadi
widened. "I bet it'll land there. Keep quiet. We've got
to stay out of sight."

The next second, Sameer shoved Ali backwards behind
a boulder, forcing him to crouch low. Just in time.

Without realising it, the boys had wandered onto the
main track through the wadi. A jeep with the top down,
thundered towards them. In it were two men, one bald,
the other bearded with a hat. And lying across the back
was the body of the leopard.

"That's them!" Sameer choked as he peered through
the branches of a tree. "The poachers!"

Sameer looked at Ali's face. Beneath the grime, his skin was drained of all colour.

"We're gonna die!" Ali moaned.

"Hush!" Sameer hissed, and the two boys didn't breathe as the men drove past.

But then suddenly, the jeep stopped and one man jumped out. "Hey boys!" he cried and he headed towards them.

"Run!" Sameer cried and once again, Ali obeyed. Terror fuzzed his brain. He ducked along a narrow side gully, but there wasn't time to look for a hiding spot. The wind was really strong now and the sand got in their mouths and eyes and hair. All they could do was run and run and run.

Then Ali fell. He collapsed from sheer exhaustion, from the bee poison, and from fear overload. Sameer sank down beside him, trying to prop them both up. The men hadn't turned the corner yet. Somehow he had to save Ali. He had to. With the last of his strength, he dragged Ali behind some rocks and threw some palm fronds across him. Then he staggered back on the path and kept on jogging to lead the poachers away.

Chapter 4

"Hey, kid. Are you OK?"

Sameer tried to focus on the voice. He felt strong arms supporting his weight. Someone was leading him to a rock.

"Sit down. Rest a bit. Then tell me what happened." The deep voice seemed a long way away. And there was something wrong with what it was saying. Rest! That was it. He couldn't rest! He had to save Ali!

Sameer jerked to his feet and looked around wildly. Where was he? A man in a red shirt crouched beside him. There were several tents set up around a water hole. Next to it was the helicopter.

He must have gone right round in a circle. How long had he been running?

"Where am I?" he managed to say through thick lips, then choked as the next moment the two poachers in the jeep drove into the campsite. Sameer stared in horror. Ali was slumped between them!

"Hey, Jack," the bald man called as he got out of the jeep and picked Ali up in his arms. "Look what I found. This little guy was hidden beside the track. He tried to grab my legs as I walked past. Would've missed him otherwise. Then he went and fainted when I grabbed him."

Sameer's head spun. Ali tried to save him! Now they were both going to die. But not if he could help it. He yelled a battle cry and charged at the man. Suddenly he tripped on a rock and lay sprawled in the dust, trying not to cry. He'd failed.

"What's your problem?" Jack said, helping Sameer to his feet. "We're just trying to help."

The bald-headed man let Ali down gently onto
the ground and felt his forehead. "Better get help.
The kid's a mess."

"Help?" Sameer thought to himself. "You don't get
help for someone you're about to kill. Do you?"

"Better get you checked out too," Bald Head
told Sameer. "Crazy kids. Why were you two running
away like that? If you'd slipped on those slopes, you
could've been killed."

"What?" Sameer couldn't believe his ears.

"Did you know you were running around leopard territory? If you blundered too near her cubs", he pointed to the limp body in the jeep, "she could have attacked you. Luckily we got to her first."

Then Sameer's anger came back. This was not his fault. There was no excuse at all to kill such a beautiful animal.

Then a lady carrying a big first-aid kit came towards them. She knelt next to Ali and touched his face gently. One eye was swollen and red. "His name?" she asked, without looking up.

"Ali," Sameer told her.

"Wake up, Ali." She tapped him firmly on the shoulder. "Wake up!"

Ali groaned, coughed and squinted around in confusion.

She probed his bruises with gentle fingers, then said: "You'll be fine. Nothing a good night's sleep won't cure."

Sameer crouched beside his brother and put his arm around him. The lady turned to Sameer and touched his forehead. "Nasty gash," she said. "It may need a stitch or two. Are your parents around? They'll have to sign a consent form."

"Yes, I want to talk to your parents too," the bearded poacher added. "Didn't they see the signs?"

"Signs?"

"They're all along the track, son. WARNING. LEOPARDS SIGHTED IN THIS AREA."

"But we came up the other side," Sameer told him. "We didn't see anything."

"You climbed the cliffs?" the bearded man said with a hint of respect. "That's tough going."

"Why did you shoot the leopard?" Ali asked in a tiny voice. "It's so beautiful."

"She's not dead," the bearded man said. "We tranquillised her."

Ali and Sameer looked up in surprise.

"The leopardess was injured. We had to help her. Also we want to tag her so we can keep track of her in the wild."

"So you're not poachers?" Sameer asked.

"Is that what you thought? That you'd seen poachers kill a leopard?"

Sameer nodded solemnly.

Bald Head laughed. "No wonder you were running away. I guess I'd have done the same in your shoes."

"But why did you chase us, then?" Sameer asked.

"We weren't sure how many leopards were around. Although it was most likely that a mother and her cubs would be alone, we couldn't be sure. We wanted to warn you to be careful."

Ali and Sameer stared at each other. There was no killing. They hadn't been chased by poachers. The scrapes, the scratches, the snake, the bees, the fear had all been for nothing! Ali's lip began to quiver. The relief was almost too much. Sameer hugged him roughly. They were OK. They were safe. He hadn't failed his little brother after all.

"So you like leopards, do you?" the bearded man said, coming over carrying a sack.

The boys nodded.

"What about cubs?" He opened the bag and three squirming leopard cubs mewled up at them.

Ali gasped in delight.

"Do you want to hold one?"

"Can we?" Sameer asked in wonder. "Won't their mother get upset?"

"You're right, she will," the bearded man said.
"We were hoping to help the leopardess on the
mountain and not have to touch her cubs at all,"
he said. "But she was hurt much more than we'd
first thought. Her injuries may take days to heal and
the cubs would've died without her. Now that we've
handled them, their mother won't take them back.
So we have to look after them from now on."

The man placed one tiny cub in Ali's lap where it nuzzled his leg. The blotchy yellowy-white fur was soft and Ali stroked it gently.

"It's about ten days old. See, its eyes are just open." He placed another one in Sameer's arms. It wriggled and sucked on his shirt.

"They're thirsty. Want to feed them?"

"How?" Ali asked.

"With this. It's special leopard-milk formula,"
Jack said, coming over with bottles of milk. He rubbed
the teat in Ali's cub's mouth and it latched onto
it hungrily. "Hold the bottle up to keep the milk
flowing," he advised.

He gave another bottle to Sameer, and the two boys
watched in wonderment as the baby leopards fed.
They must have been really thirsty because they
finished the milk in minutes.

Finally Jack said, "Well boys, it's time for you to go back to your parents or they'll get worried. I'll drive you if you like."

Ali and Sameer reluctantly handed back the tiny animals.

Jack saw how gentle they were. He smiled and said, "Once you boys have got cleaned up, how would you like to come back later today and feed them again for us? You could come tomorrow too, and for as long as we're here. It'd be a big help for us to know they were in good hands."

Ali and Sameer stared at each other in amazement. They'd been scratched and torn, slithered and crawled over, been bitten and lost. They were bleeding, bruised and swollen. Did they now want to play nurse to leopard cubs?

Of course they did!

Map of the mountains

✿ Ideas for guided reading ✿

Learning objectives: compare the usefulness of techniques such as prediction and empathy in exploring the meaning of texts; tell a story using notes and techniques such as repetition, recap, humour; explore how writers use language for dramatic effects

Curriculum links: Citizenship: Living in a diverse world;

Geography: The mountain environment

Interest words: Arabian, scorpion, poisonous, mutant, relented, receding, wadi, tranquillised, festering, camel spider

Resources: globe or map, writing and art materials, caption cards

Getting started

This book can be read over two or more guided reading sessions.

- Look at the front and back cover together and ask children questions to stimulate discussion. *What do you think the story is about? Where do you think the story is set?*

- Explain that the story is set in Arabia. Find out if any of the children know where Arabia is and ask them to point to it on a map or globe. Ask questions to stimulate discussion, e.g. *What kind of landscape would you find there? What is the weather like there?*

- Ask children to name stories from other cultures they have read, e.g. Anansi stories, etc.

Reading and responding

- Ask a child to read pp2-3 aloud. Discuss what has been read and ask questions, e.g. *What have you learnt about the characters of Sameer and Ali so far?*

- Encourage children to read the first two chapters in pairs, making notes about the characters and how they behave.